BERTIE

Based on *The Railway Series* by the Rev. W. Awdry

D0532867

Illustrations by
Robin Davies

EGMONT

EGMONT

We bring stories to life

First published in Great Britain 2004
This edition published 2007
by Egmont UK Limited
239 Kensington High Street, London W8 6SA
All Rights Reserved

Thomas the Tank Engine & Friends™

A BRITT ALLCROFT COMPANY PRODUCTION

Based on The Railway Series by The Reverend W Awdry
© 2007 Gullane (Thomas) LLC. A HIT Entertainment Company

Thomas the Tank Engine & Friends and Thomas & Friends are trademarks of Gullane (Thomas) Limited.
Thomas the Tank Engine & Friends and Design is Reg. US. Pat. & Tm. Off.

ISBN 978 1 4052 3203 6
1 3 5 7 9 10 8 6 4 2

Printed in China

TO THE TRAINS ➞

This is a story about Bertie the Bus. Bertie and Thomas both think they can go fastest. They just can't agree, so they decide to have a race to settle the argument once and for all . . .

One day, Thomas was waiting at the junction when a bus came into the Yard.

"Hello," said Thomas. "Who are you?"

"I'm Bertie. Who are you?"

"I'm Thomas. I run this branch line."

"Ah – I remember now," said Bertie. "You were stuck in the snow. I took your passengers, and Terence the Tractor pulled you out. I've come to help you with your passengers today."

"Help me?" said Thomas crossly. "I don't need any help. Anyway, I can go faster than you."

"You can't," said Bertie.

"I can," huffed Thomas.

"I'll race you," said Bertie.

Their Drivers agreed to the race.

"Are you ready?" said the Stationmaster. "Go!"

And they were off . . .

Thomas always had to start off slowly, and Bertie was soon ahead of him. But Thomas didn't hurry.

"Why don't you go fast? Why don't you go fast?" called Annie and Clarabel, anxiously.

"Wait and see! Wait and see!" hissed Thomas.

"He's a long way ahead, a long way ahead," they wailed.

But Thomas didn't mind. He remembered the level crossing.

Bertie was there, waiting impatiently at the gates while Thomas and his carriages went sailing through.

"Goodbye, Bertie," called Thomas.

After that, the road left the railway, so Thomas, Annie and Clarabel couldn't see Bertie. Then they had to stop at a station to let some passengers off.

"Peep, pip, peep! Quickly, please!" called Thomas.

Everybody got out quickly, the Guard blew his whistle and off they went again.

"Come along. Come along," sang Thomas.

"We're coming along. We're coming along!" sang Annie and Clarabel.

"Hurry! Hurry! Hurry!" panted Thomas.

Then he looked ahead and saw Bertie crossing the bridge over the railway, tooting triumphantly on his horn!

"Oh, deary me! Oh, deary me!" groaned Thomas.

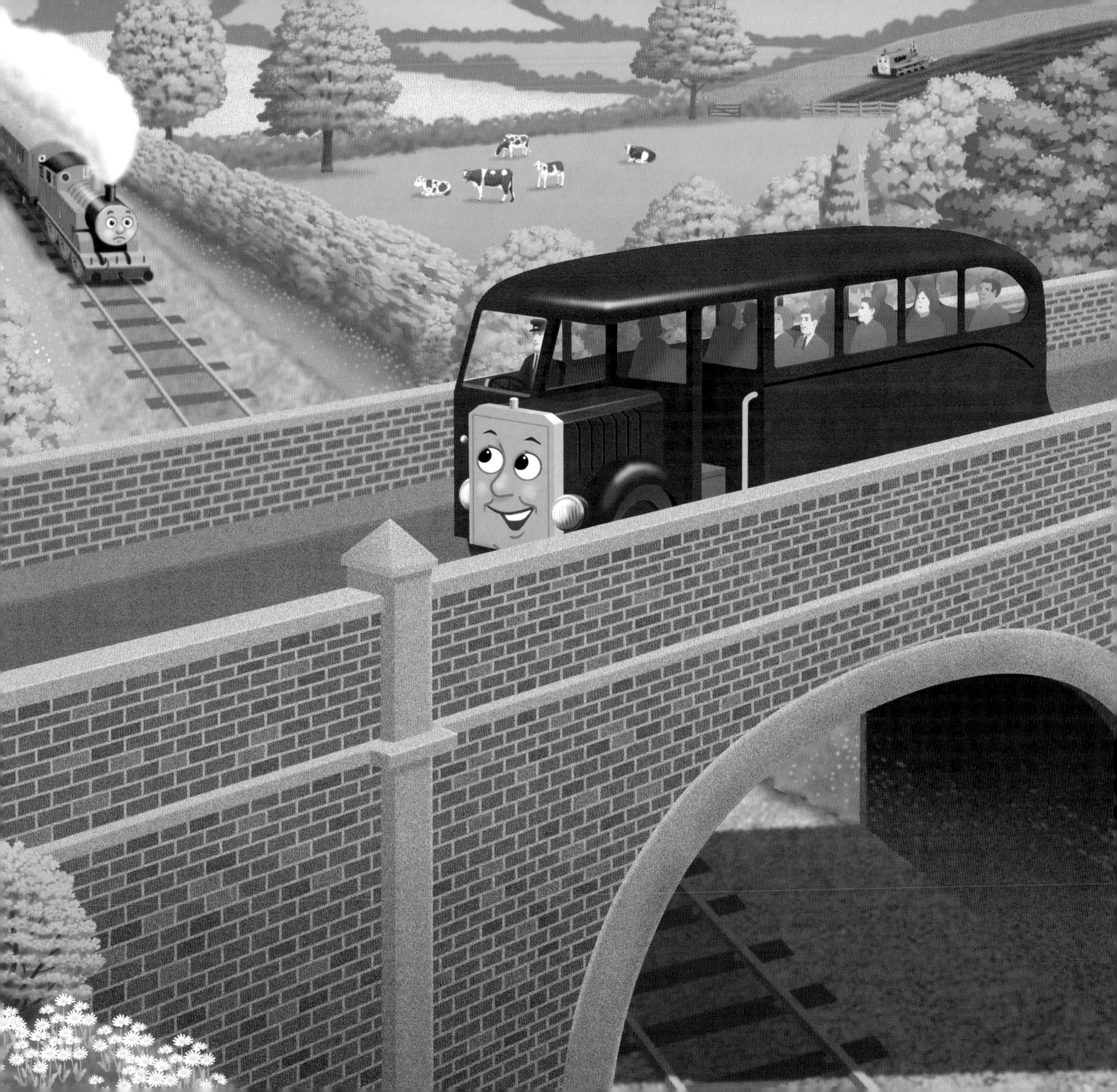

"Steady, Thomas," said his Driver. "We'll beat Bertie yet."

"We'll beat Bertie yet. We'll beat Bertie yet," echoed Annie and Clarabel.

"We'll do it. We'll do it," panted Thomas. "Oh, bother, there's a station."

As Thomas stopped, he heard a toot.

"Goodbye, Thomas," called Bertie. "You must be tired. Sorry I can't stop – we buses have to work, you know. Goodbye!"

The next station was by the river. They got there quickly, but the signal was up.

"Oh, dear," thought Thomas. "We've lost!"

But at the station he had a drink of water and felt much better.

Then the signal dropped.

"Hurrah, we're off! Hurrah, we're off!" puffed Thomas happily.

As Thomas crossed the bridge, he heard an impatient "Toot! Toot!"

There was Bertie, waiting at the traffic lights.

But as soon as the lights changed, Bertie started with a roar, and chased after Thomas.

Now Thomas reached his full speed. Bertie tried hard, but Thomas was too fast.

Whistling joyfully, he plunged into the tunnel, leaving Bertie far behind.

"I've done it. I've done it," panted Thomas.

"We've done it, hooray! We've done it, hooray!" chanted Annie and Clarabel, as they whooshed into the last station.

The passengers all cheered loudly. When Bertie came in, they also gave him a big welcome.

"Well done, Thomas," said Bertie. "That was fun, but I would have to grow wings like an aeroplane to beat you over that hill!"

Thomas and Bertie now keep each other busy. Bertie finds people who want to travel by train and takes them to Thomas, while Thomas brings people to the station for Bertie to take home.

They often talk about their race. But Bertie's passengers don't like being bounced around like peas in a pan, and The Fat Controller has told Thomas not to race at dangerous speeds.

So although (between you and me) they would like to have another race, I don't think they ever will. Do you?

Collect the other characters in the Thomas Audio range:

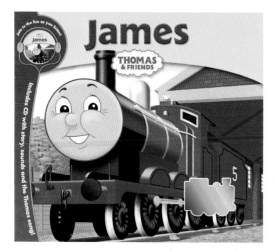

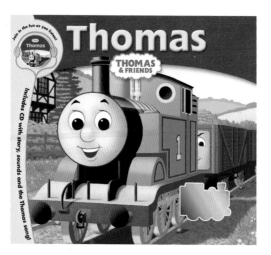

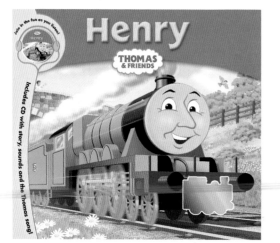

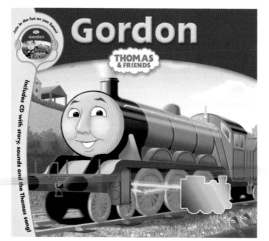